A.J. Cosmo

silly stories, important lessons

D1501665

Written by:
A.J. Cosmo

Illustrated by:
A.J. Cosmo

Editor:
Angela Pearson

Book Layout:
Ricardo Aldape

Production:
Thought Bubble Publishing

The Monster That Ate My Socks

A.J. Cosmo

Something was eating my socks.

I would go through two pairs of socks every day: One pair I wore to school and one pair for soccer practice.

Every morning I would wake up and one or two of my dirty socks would be gone.

"What are you doing with your socks?" Mom would ask.

I got in trouble because my Mom hated buying more socks.

One morning when I was putting my pajamas in the dirty clothes hamper, I noticed a little piece of torn cloth. It was wet and had bite marks. It looked like a piece of chewed sock.

I would have blamed our dog, but we didn't have one! I showed Mom, but she didn't believe me.

"You need to take care of your socks!" she said before sending me off to school.

That night, I laid my dirty socks out on the floor. I pretended to fall asleep while I watched over the side of the bed. Around midnight the door to my room creaked open and a little green face peeked into the room. The creature had three eyes and a big mouth filled with teeth. It was so fat its little legs could barely hold it up. It walked on all fours, its long arms moving it across the carpet.

I pulled the covers up so it wouldn't see me.

The monster sniffed the air, licked its lips, and rubbed its hands together.

It picked up the first sock. It devoured the sock like it was candy. It rubbed its belly and ate another one. Soon enough it had eaten all four of the socks.

I leapt out of bed and grabbed the monster. It let out a horrible squeal and fought back. We wrestled on the ground. It tried to bite and claw me.

Mom knocked on the door. "What is all that noise?"

The monster got away and ran into the closet just as Mom opened the bedroom door.

"Shouldn't you be asleep?" Mom asked.

"There was a monster eating my socks!" I cried.

"Tomorrow is a school day, mister!" Mom said as she wagged her finger.

"But the monster is in the closet!" I yelled as I pointed as hard as I could.

My mom walked over and looked in the closet. The clever monster was hiding under the toys.

"There's no monster here, young man. Now go to bed."

"Mom, there really is a monster!"

She spotted a bit of sock that had fallen out of the monster's mouth.

"No more destroying your socks, you hear me? This has got to stop," she said as she picked up a smelly sock. "We spend too much money on socks!"

I knew she wouldn't believe me, so I just said goodnight.

Quietly, I checked the closet, but the monster was not there. It must have gotten away.

At school the next day, I talked to my friends about the monster. No one believed me, except for my best friend, Ryan. He said he had seen the monster before and it loved to eat dirty socks.

"The dirtier the better. I saw him after I got back from camp, when I had a whole backpack full of dirty clothes," said Ryan.

"So what should I do?" I asked.

Ryan shrugged. "Maybe we could make a trap and bait it with socks. Do you think that would work?"

We made a plan together. I would invite Ryan over to spend the night, and we would make a monster trap.

Ryan came over the next night. He brought a backpack full of dirty socks. We were going to give the monster a feast!

We tied a string to a ruler and used it to prop up a laundry basket. We setup the trap over a huge pile of socks. We hid under the covers of the bed and waited for the monster to appear.

Everyone was asleep except Ryan and me when the monster peeked into the room and looked around. It looked scared, like it might be caught again, but the smell of the dirty socks was too much for him.

We watched as it crept around the room to the trap, and picked up a smelly sock. We pulled the string. The ruler flew out and the basket fell down with a thud.

We jumped off the bed onto the floor.

The monster rolled around in the basket, barking and squealing.

"It's going to wake everybody up!" I whispered. I reached under the basket and grabbed the monster. It squealed in my arms and I thought I heard Mom wake up.

Ryan shoved a huge wad of socks into the monster's mouth.

"There. Now what do we do with it?" I asked as I held the monster tight. It struggled to break free but still managed to chew the socks.

"We need a cage," my friend said as he looked around the room. He took his backpack and dumped out the contents. I shoved the monster in the bag and we zipped it tight. It wiggled around inside for a few minutes.

"Let me go!" It suddenly growled.

Ryan and I were surprised.

"Why are you eating my socks?" I asked.

"They are delicious," said the monster.

"It's getting me in trouble," I growled.

"I cannot help it," said the monster as he shrugged. "They smell like sweat and feet! They are stinky and wet!"

Ryan gagged. The way the monster loved smelly feet was disgusting.

"Why don't you eat someone else's socks?" I said.

"Your socks are the most tasty," said the monster as he shifted around in the backpack. "Something smell good in here, tasty."

"I'm going to wake up Mom," I said.
"No!" the monster wailed.

"Why not?" I asked in no mood to listen to a monster's nonsense.

"If the adults know then they will destroy us!"

"Good!"

"No, not good- bad! We don't mean any harm. We are just hungry," begged the monster.

"We? There are more of you?" I asked.

"Yes. I have little ones, little ones hungry for smelly socks."

My heart sank. I couldn't hurt someone with a family, even if it was a monster. What was I supposed to do? If the monster ate my socks, I would get in trouble. If the monster had no socks to eat, his family would be hungry.

"Can we see your family?" Ryan asked. The monster thought for a moment.

"Yes, but only if you promise not to tell," he said.

"We promise," Ryan and I said together.

With the monster in Ryan's backpack, we snuck out of the house. Out back, far from the house, Ryan set down the backpack and unzipped the zipper.

"Don't you dare run away," I said.

The monster waddled out of the backpack and looked up at me. I was waiting for him to bolt out of there.

"This way," he said as he pointed.

The monster led us to a clearing in the forest behind my home. A little hole was hidden underneath a rotten log.

"Come out." The monster called.
Three little monsters crawled out. They were tiny, no bigger than my hand, and they had big adorable eyes.

One of the little monsters stood up and begged like a dog asking for a treat.

The other one stayed mostly hidden and whimpered.

"They are hungry. I have been gone for a long time," said the monster.

They were so cute. I couldn't imagine harming them.

"I don't think I could stand to see these guys starve," said Ryan.

"Me neither," I replied.

Ryan and I took off our socks and gave them to the little monsters. They ate the socks up, every thread.

"What are we supposed to do?" I asked. "We can't keep feeding you socks, we will run out!"

However the monster wasn't listening. Instead it sniffed the air and put its hand on my leg.

"Something smells delicious," said the monster.

"You already ate all of our socks," Ryan said.

"No, this is not socks. It smells different. It is full of mistakes," said the monster.

"Full of mistakes?" I asked, confused.

"He means my homework," Ryan said.

"Your homework?" I asked.

"Yeah, I hide it in the front pocket. This hasn't been my best year," Ryan said.

"Do you mind?" I asked.

"Be my guest," Ryan shrugged.

The monsters gathered around as I looked through the pockets. Sure enough, there was a wad of papers stuffed in the front.

There were math pages with red ink marking mistakes, and a spelling test with most of the words spelled wrong.

"Are those F's?" The monster said as it licked its lips.

"Yeah," Ryan said as he turned red with embarrassment.

"Can they eat them?" I asked.

Ryan shrugged. "I guess so," he said. "Maybe I should do better in school."

The monsters ate my friend's homework. They loved it!

"That was delicious. We are all full now," said the monster with a burp.

"That's good, but what about tomorrow? We can't keep feeding you socks and homework!" I said.

I mean, not that I would have minded having a monster for a pet. In all seriousness though, there was no way that a smelly-footed boy like myself and a bad student like Ryan could keep a family of four fed.

We spent the weekend feeding the rest of Ryan's bad homework to the monsters.

On Monday, I took two backpacks with me. At the end of the day, the bell rang and I stayed behind as the kids lined up and left the classroom. I took out the second backpack and let the monsters out. The big monster and all three little monsters ran out and sniffed around the room.

"What is this place?" The monster asked.

"This is my classroom. This is where all of the bad homework comes from," I said.

The monster ran to the trash can.

"I see! This metal log is full of bad!" The babies ran over and pulled all the bad homework the students had thrown away.

The monster looked like it was going to cry with joy.

"Why do this for us?" the monster asked. "Why be nice?"

I shrugged. "I guess because everyone needs a home, right?" I said. "And I need my socks."

"Thank you." The monster said. The monster hugged me and the little monsters did, too.

"If you need anything, I will be here every day in class. Just say "Hi" during recess." "Recess?" asked the monster.

"Recess is when everyone goes out on the playground," I said. "I'll stay behind when I can and check on you."

"You should be able to hide in the closet during the day and at night, when everyone is gone, you have the whole classroom to yourself," added Ryan.

The monster nodded. I guess monsters are naturally good at hiding.

We said our goodbyes and I left for soccer practice.

Mom was happy that my socks had finally stopped disappearing. Well, most of them. Sometimes I left dirty socks for the monsters in the recycling bin as a treat every other week.

The teacher never noticed the monsters, except for the occasional knocked over trash can. The other kids loved having the monsters there, because they made their bad grades on homework easier to hide.

They lived happily ever after, and I never saw the monster again.

Or so I thought...

The End

Lesson Plan

by Martin Tiller

Possible Unknown or Difficult Words:

- Hamper
- Midnight
- Devoured
- Squeal
- Feast
- Wailed
- Occasional

Before reading, preview the Text:
(Ask readers prediction questions.)

What do you think this story is about?
What tells you that?
What do the illustrations tell you?

After reading:
(Ask guiding questions.)

"What do you think is the main idea of this story?"
"Why would the author write this story?"
"Who are the characters in this story?"
"What is the setting of this story?"

Have the student sequence the story in Beginning, Middle, and End format. Checking to make sure they put information in order.

Have the student write a summary of the story in their own words.

Word Work:

From the word sock what are other words that end in –ock?
(stock, rock, lock, clock, mock, shock, chock, flock…)

What other words can you make that begin with squ like squeal?
(square, squirm, squish, squash…)

What are other words you can make with the "ate" word chunk?
(hate, mate, late, plate, fate…)

....

Follow Martin @mctiller
www.martintiller.com
email: http://eepurl.com/1EWcT

More From A. J. Cosmo

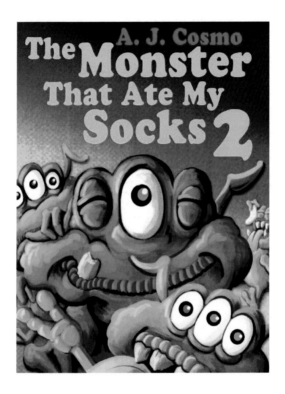

All is well at the school until textbooks start
disappearing... Something has been eating all of
the wood at school and it's up to our hero
to find out why the sock monster suddenly
changed his diet!

Available on Amazon.com and
other fine retailers!

My stories are crafted to help parents teach their children simple everyday lessons in an easy to understand manner. By artfully marrying beautiful illustrations and language, I challenge children to explore my magical worlds. Written for the transitional reader, my stories allow your child to develop and master a new level of reading.

A.J. Cosmo

73492896R00018

Made in the USA
Lexington, KY
09 December 2017